NEVER TRUMPET with a CRUMPET

Amy Gibson

Illustrated by
Jenn Harney

BOYDS MILLS PRESS
An Imprint of Highlights
Honesdale, Pennsylvania

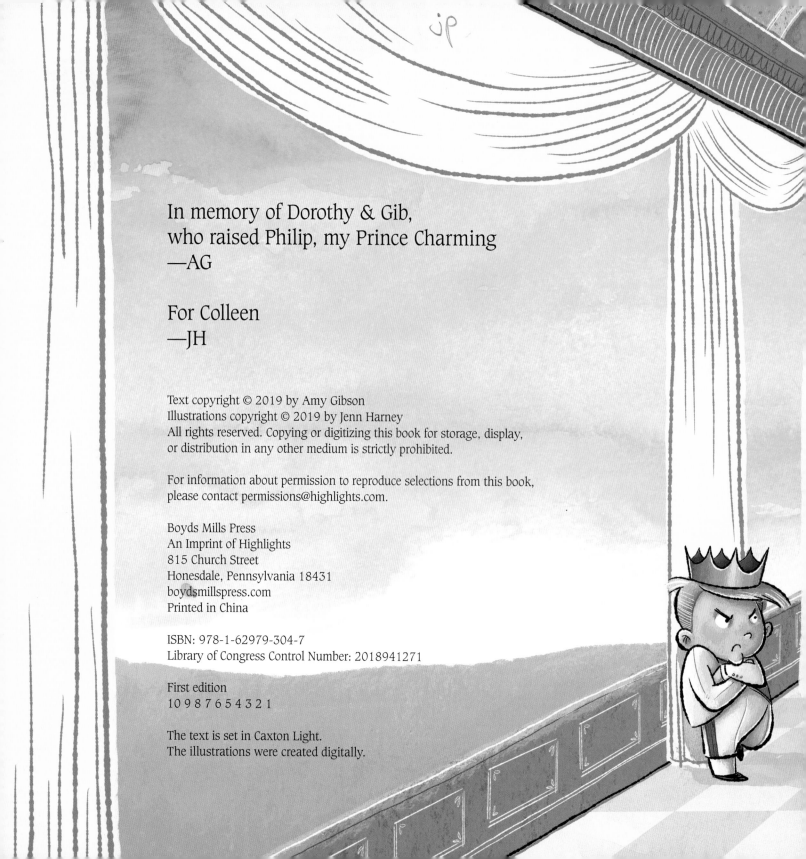

In memory of Dorothy & Gib,
who raised Philip, my Prince Charming
—AG

For Colleen
—JH

Boyds Mills Press
An Imprint of Highlights
815 Church Street
Honesdale, Pennsylvania 18431
boydsmillspress.com
Printed in China

ISBN: 978-1-62979-304-7
Library of Congress Control Number: 2018941271

First edition
10 9 8 7 6 5 4 3 2 1

The text is set in Caxton Light.
The illustrations were created digitally.

Now if perchance Her Majesty
so happens to ask *you* to tea,
it's time to press your Sunday best.
She'll put your manners to the test.

Curtsy. Speak when spoken to:
"Your Majesty, how do you do?"

Nod to greet The Prince and Duke;
don't bend at flipper, fin, or fluke.

Sit up straight. Don't slump. Don't slouch.
Lay your napkin on your pouch.

Have patience. Let your hostess pour.
One lump or two—not three or four.

Do say, "Thank you." Do say, "Please."
Cover if you cough or sneeze.

Sip your tea. Don't lap it up.
No blowing bubbles in your cup.

Show courtesy. Don't take too much,
but always take the one you touch.

No wolfing food or snapping jaws.
Use your fork and not your paws.

Resist the urge to lick your chin.
Choose silverware from outside in.

And—goodness, gracious!—never trumpet
when you're nibbling on a crumpet.

Try *one* bite of foods you hate.
No hiding crusts beneath your plate.

Dainty bites! Please chew your food.
But never chew the cud—that's rude.

Oh, *do* sit still. Refrain from spills.
Mind your antlers. Watch your quills.

No reaching, grabbing—mercy me!—
however long your tongue may be.

Leave elbows off the table, dear.
No swinging from the chandelier.

Don't drain your teacup to the dregs.
And NEVER gnaw the table legs.

If you know just what to do,
and thank your hostess when you're through,
Her Majesty will be impressed
to dine with such a lovely guest.

Then as you go your merry way,
The Queen will smile and wave and say,
"It's such a pity you can't stay.
Do come for tea another day."